The Wish Fairy
The Treasure Trap

ALSO BY LISA ANN SCOTT

The Wish Fairy

ENCHANTED PONY ACADEMY

The Wish Fairy
The Treasure Trap

Lisa Ann Scott

illustrated by
Heather Burns

SCHOLASTIC INC.

ISBN 978-1-338-12100-1

10 9 8 7 6 5 4 3 2 1   18 19 20 21 22

Printed in the U.S.A.   40

First printing 2018

Book design by Yaffa Jaskoll

To my second-grade teacher,
Suzanne Langworthy, who launched
my love of reading and writing.
You made me want to be a writer!

Chapter 1

Brooke bounced on her toes, excited to make her third wish. A real wish—which was really going to come true, from a real fairy!

The day before, Brooke's cat, Patches, had tried to catch a dragonfly. But it turned out to not be a bug at all—it was a fairy named Calla! And because Brooke saved the fairy's life, she was granted wishes—seven of them!

She had to use them all in one fortnight,

though. It was the rule of Calla's land, Fairvana, which was hidden deep in the woods behind Brooke's house.

The first two had been a bit of a disaster, but this third wish was *perfect*.

"Only five wishes left," Calla said, zipping around in the air above Brooke and her best friend, Izzy. "Use them wisely."

They sat behind Izzy's house. Brooke petted Patches and thought.

Brooke's first wish had been for one hundred cats, her very favorite animal. All of those kitties had been so cute, but they were a lot of work. Even worse, it had turned out that almost all of them already belonged to other people! Missing cat flyers had popped up all over town.

So Brooke had used her second wish to return all the cats to their homes. All but one, that is. Sweet little Pumpkin had been a stray, so Izzy asked her parents if she could keep her as a pet—and they said yes!

The biggest problem, though, had been Brooke's cat, Patches. The black kitty with white spots had run away, frightened by all the new felines. Brooke had thought she was gone forever until they found her hiding at Izzy's house.

So this time, Brooke was going to get things exactly right. She didn't want to hurt anyone with her next wish.

"So, what's it going to be?" Izzy asked.

"It's the perfect wish. I just know it," Brooke said.

"What, what, what?" Izzy spun in circles until she tumbled onto the ground.

Brooke giggled. "Be patient, you'll see."

"Remember, be careful what you wish for!" Calla said, pirouetting through the air. The tiny fairy was just a few inches tall and could move as fast as a hummingbird.

Brooke took a deep breath, practiced a few times in her head, and then announced, "Calla, I wish for long-lost buried gold to appear in my meadow."

Izzy held up her hand and the two friends slapped a high five. "That's perfect!"

"I know! If it's long-lost gold that's buried right now, no one's going to miss it," Brooke said. "And I can use it to buy whatever I want!"

Izzy pumped her arm in the air. "Woo-hoo! You're going to be rich!"

"Is that *exactly* what you wish?" Calla asked.

Brooke thought about her words and was certain she had gotten it right. "Yes, Calla. That's my wish."

"Very well," Calla said. A glittery flash filled the air around them. "Your wish has been granted."

Brooke shrieked with joy and dashed to the meadow. She shielded her eyes from the sun, scanning the field of flowers and grass looking for a bag or trunk or pile of gold. She and Izzy ran back and forth across the meadow, searching. But they didn't see any gold.

They stood on the big rock in the middle of the field for a better view. Calla was lounging on the rock, crafting flower petals into a skirt.

Brooke bent down to her. "Where is it?"

"I don't know."

Brooke sighed. "But I asked for it to be in

the meadow, and I've looked for it every-where. Why can't I find it, Calla?"

Calla shrugged. "Probably because you're looking above ground. You asked for long-lost *buried* gold."

Chapter 2

Brooke blinked at Calla a few times in disbelief. "You mean the gold is *buried* in the meadow?"

Calla nodded. "That's what you asked for—buried gold."

Brooke shook her head. "No, no, no. I meant I wanted gold that *was* buried somewhere else to appear in my meadow. Not to be buried *here*."

"You should have said so." Calla fastened the flower petal skirt around her dress.

Brooke groaned. Had she messed up another wish?

"Don't worry—we'll find it." Izzy grabbed Brooke's hand. "Let's go up in the tree house so we can see the whole field at once. Maybe we'll spot some clues about where it is."

"Good idea," Brooke said.

They bounded across the meadow, their two cats following close behind. Calla zoomed along overhead.

"I told you to be perfectly specific with your wishes!"

"I thought I was!" Brooke said. Who knew making wishes would be so difficult?

The girls climbed the rope ladder onto the platform of the tree house. Brooke dashed inside and searched the trunk where they kept their adventure gear: buckets and jars for collecting treasures, a telescope for gazing at the stars, a mega-phone so they could shout across the field, old sheets for sleepovers and picnics.

"Here they are!" She grabbed the binoculars they used to watch birds and other creatures. Just the night before, Calla had shown Brooke and Izzy the glowing blue wisps that lived in the magical forest.

"Look for a mound of dirt," Izzy suggested. "Or an area where the grass isn't growing?"

Brooke scanned the meadow with the binoculars, but nothing seemed out of place. What was she going to do?

Calla curled up on the tiny bed they'd brought from Brooke's dollhouse. She yawned. "Wake me up when you find it."

Brooke looked back and forth across the meadow for some sort of clue, but nothing seemed unusual. Then something caught her eye. Not far from the creek, there was a bare patch in the grass. It looked like fresh dirt. She hadn't noticed it the day before.

"I think I found it!" She scrambled down the ladder. Izzy, the cats, and Calla were close behind her.

"I'm a faster runner. I'll get the shovel out of your shed," Izzy said.

"Thanks!" Brooke headed for the creek, while Izzy got the shovel. Brooke's heart raced, hoping this really was the spot where the gold was buried.

Patches curled around Brooke's legs as she examined the spot. She scooped the cat up in her arms. "I'll get you a magnificent kitty bed with my gold! If I can find it."

Izzy raced back with the shovel. "Here! Hurry! I can't wait to see how much there is!"

Brooke set down Patches and placed the shovel against the ground. She used one foot to force it into the earth. She removed a scoop of dirt, then another and another. Her legs and shoulders began to ache from the hard work.

She swiped the back of her hand against her sweaty forehead. "Maybe this isn't the spot."

"Let me dig for a while." Izzy took the shovel and dug until there was a deep hole in front of them, but there was still no sign of the gold.

"Oh no. How are we going to find it?"

Brooke nervously bit her lip, looking back at the rest of the meadow.

"You could make a wish for me to find it for you," Calla offered.

"No! I don't want to waste any more wishes," Brooke said.

"Should we get a metal detector?" Izzy asked.

"That would be great, but I don't have any money. We spent it all on cat food." Brooke sighed.

"Right," Izzy said.

Brooke was tired and thirsty, but she wasn't ready to give up yet. "I'm going to dig a little bit deeper. It has to be here. I didn't notice this bare spot yesterday. Why else would it suddenly appear?"

The hole was soon deep enough that she climbed into it to make it easier to dig. She scooped out another shovel full of dirt when she noticed something odd, like a scrap of fabric. She got on her hands and knees and pawed through the earth with her fingers until she could grab onto a hunk of material. "I think I found it!"

Chapter 3

Brooke scooped away the rest of the dirt and pulled out a small bag. Her shoulders slumped. "That's it?"

"Guess you should have added, 'A *lot* of buried gold,'" Calla said. "So many important wish lessons are being learned on this adventure! While it certainly is shameful to be discovered by humans, this experience will be so very valuable when I return home to share what I've learned. Perhaps I'll write a book. *The Amazing Calla, Human Expert.* There will be a giant picture of me on the cover." Calla tapped her tiny finger against her chin, thinking.

Izzy slapped a hand over her mouth to cover her laughter.

Brooke was too exhausted to chuckle.

She set the bag on the ground and climbed out of the hole.

"Federal Bank of Morristown," she said, reading the faded name printed on the bag. "That's our town."

"Open it!" Izzy said.

With shaky fingers, Brooke untied the rope holding the bag closed. She peered inside. The bag was filled with shiny gold coins. She plucked one from the pile and held it up. On one side, there was a picture of an eagle and the words "United States of America." She flipped it over and saw a picture of a lady's head. "Liberty, 1801."

"Wow! That's really old."

"Good! I wanted long-lost gold that doesn't belong to anyone."

"I wonder how much this is worth?" Izzy asked.

Brooke turned the coin over in her hand. "It doesn't say on the coin."

"Let's count how many there are," Izzy suggested.

Together, they dumped the bag on the ground and piled them into stacks of ten.

"We've got fifteen stacks of ten," Brooke said. "And two leftover."

Izzy did the math in her head. "That's a hundred and fifty-two coins. You can probably get a lot of cool stuff with that. It's gold!"

Patches sniffed the stacks of coins and knocked one over with her paw.

Brooke laughed. "Let's go to the store and see how much we can buy with one."

"Can you purchase more chocolate chips
and sugar cubes?" Calla asked. "And while I
love my new bed, I could really use a table
and chairs in the tree house, too."

"Of course, Calla! I'll buy you lots of
wonderful things." Brooke held out a finger,
and Calla flew over and perched on it.

"You are a most kind human," she said. "I'll have a special chapter on you in my book."

"Aww, thank you."

"You should make a list of everything you want to get," Izzy said. "Let me grab my notebook."

While Izzy ran back to the tree house, Brooke cleaned up in the creek, washing the dirt and grime off her hands and legs. She petted Patches. "You and Pumpkin have to stay here."

Patches seemed to agree and curled up under a shrub by the creek. Pumpkin joined her.

When Izzy returned, they dropped the money bag in her backpack and walked into town. Izzy took notes as Brooke listed all the things she wanted to buy: a fancy cat bed for Patches, and one for Pumpkin, too. Elegant canopy beds for Brooke and Izzy. Arts-and-craft supplies, and of course books.

"That's a good start," Brooke said.

"This is so exciting!" Izzy was walking so fast Brooke could barely keep up.

Calla hid in the pocket of Brooke's shirt when they got to the store in the middle of town.

"Get whatever you want, Izzy!" Brooke grabbed a shopping cart, and they headed for the candy aisle.

"I shouldn't," Izzy said. "You know how bad sugar is for me."

"Right. I'm sorry," Brooke said. "Let's head over to the craft section."

The girls laughed as they cleared the shelves of all the drawing pads and colored pencils. Then Brooke chose the biggest, most expensive pack of markers the store had.

"We should get all these canvases and make paintings for the tree house!" Izzy said. She added blank canvases, paints, and brushes to the cart. It was almost overflowing now. They looked at each other and giggled again.

Brooke stopped in the toy aisle and added a few tiny dollhouse items. "Those are for you!" she whispered to Calla.

"You're such a generous human. How in the world am I going to bring this all back to Fairvana?" Calla asked from Brooke's pocket.

They pushed the cart to the register and the store owner, Mrs. Smith, widened her eyes. "That's a very big purchase. You sure you have enough cash for that?"

Brooke pulled a gold coin out of her pocket. "Better than that, I have gold!"

Mrs. Smith scrunched her eyebrows together as she picked up the coin. "That's a very old coin. I don't think it's even accepted as legal tender these days."

"But it's gold. It's got to be worth something," Izzy said.

"Where did you girls get this?" Mrs. Smith asked.

"We found it in my meadow," Brooke explained.

A long line was growing behind them at the register.

"You found gold in your meadow? That's just over on Cherry Street, right?" Mrs. Smith's eyes got big. "Buried treasure right here in town. How amazing!"

"I know! We've got a long list of things we want to buy with it," Brooke said.

"I can see that. But I'm sorry, I can't accept this as payment. You could take it to the bank and see what it's worth. Do you have another way to pay for all this?"

Brooke frowned. "No. But we'll be right back." Brooke parked the cart at the end of the checkout lane and headed outside. "Come on, Izzy, let's go to the bank."

Chapter 4

The bank was quiet when they entered. Calla flew out of Brooke's pocket and perched on the corner of a nearby picture frame. Brooke gasped, but no one seemed to notice the fairy.

Izzy and Brooke walked up to the teller. Brooke plopped the bag and one of the coins on the counter.

"Hello," she said. "We need someone to

tell us how much these gold coins are worth, please."

The teller picked up the coin. "I've never seen one like this before. These certainly aren't in circulation now. Let me call the manager. He's an expert on old money." She set down the gold and picked up the phone.

Brooke looked at Izzy and crossed her fingers. "If we're lucky, we might have hundreds of dollars' worth of gold."

Izzy didn't answer. Brooke waved a hand in front of her friend's face until Izzy shook herself out of her daze.

"Sorry, I was just thinking what else you could do with all that money. Wouldn't a rowboat for the pond be fun? Or a bicycle built for two? And think of all the books we could buy! We wouldn't even have to check them out of the library anymore. We could have our own."

"And I could put more money in the library donation jar so they could buy more books, too," Brooke said. "Remember Mrs. Nelson said the library budget was in trouble?"

"Right! Great idea," Izzy said.

Brooke scanned the lobby for Calla. She found her examining a jar of suckers sitting on an empty desk.

Brooke was about to put Calla back in her pocket when an older man walked through the lobby toward them. "I'm Mr. Rodriguez, the bank manager. How can I help you?"

"Hi, I'm Brooke and this is Izzy. We have these gold coins and we don't know how much they're worth. Mrs. Smith at the store wouldn't take them." Nervously, Brooke tucked her hands in her shorts pockets.

Mr. Rodriguez picked up one of the coins and his jaw dropped. "I've never seen one of these in person before. They're incredibly rare. It's a Turban Head Eagle ten-dollar coin."

"Wow! And we've got a hundred and fifty-two of them!" Izzy exclaimed.

Mr. Rodriguez took a step backward and grabbed the counter. "You're kidding me."

"No, sir," Brooke said. "We found them in my meadow."

Izzy fluttered her fingers, counting. "That means you have one thousand, five hundred and twenty dollars! You can buy so many fun things!"

Mr. Rodriguez opened and closed his mouth a few times before he could say anything else. "Girls, those coins are worth a lot more than that. Like I said, they're extremely rare."

"So how much are they worth?" Brooke asked excitedly.

"At least ten-thousand dollars . . ."

Izzy gasped before he could finish.

". . . per coin."

Now *Brooke's* mouth was opening and closing without any sound coming out. Finally she said, "That's almost . . ." Numbers spun in her head, and she couldn't make sense of them.

"They're worth at least one and a half million dollars," Mr. Rodriguez said.

Izzy teetered and fell on her butt.

Brooke helped Izzy back up. "I can't believe it," she squealed. She high-fived Izzy. "Can we trade in the coins to you for all that money, Mr. Rodriguez?"

He pinched his lips together in a tight line. "Girls, I'm afraid I have bad news for you."

"What?" Brooke asked, confused.

"You can't keep this money," he said.

Brooke blinked at him. "Why not? I found it, and it was behind my house. So it should be mine." She clamped her mouth shut before she added that she had wished for it and that it was *long-lost* gold.

"But do you see the name of the bag? Federal Bank of Morristown? That's our bank. In 1801, this bank was robbed of two bags of gold coins. Just like these. The Turban Head Eagle coins."

Brooke gulped. Of course the gold had to

come from somewhere. She just didn't think anyone would still be looking for it!

"I'll call your mother, Brooke," Mr. Rodriguez said. "She needs to know what you have here."

Chapter 5

Brooke's mother said nothing for a long time. "How ever did you find this?"

Customers were gathered nearby, watching and listening.

There was no way in the world Brooke could explain. "Um . . . I saw a strange bare spot near the creek and decided to dig." She looked around the lobby, but couldn't spot Calla. *I hope she's not getting into trouble!*

Her mom stared at the coins. "Must've been there for a long time."

Brooke wished she could tell the truth. The gold coins could have been any- where before she wished them into her meadow.

Mr. Rodriguez led them to a wall along the side of the bank. He pointed to a picture. "That's an actual reward poster from 1801."

Brooke read the poster to herself:

WANTED: THE NOTORIOUS BIG, BAD BOO-HOO

BROTHERS WHO HELD UP THE FEDERAL

BANK OF MORRISTOWN ON OCTOBER 28, 1801.

$4000 IN GOLD COIN WAS TAKEN.

$500 REWARD FOR CAPTURE OF THE MEN.

$100 FOR RECOVERY OF THE GOLD COIN.

"The robbers made off with four hundred

gold coins," Mr. Rodriguez said. "I imagine you found what they hadn't yet spent."

Brooke's mom shook her head and sat down. "I can't believe it."

"I know the girls would like to keep this," Mr. Rodriguez said. "Who wouldn't? But considering that the gold is in one of our bags, the bank is going to try to reclaim it as ours. I think the best thing we can do right now is keep it in a safe deposit box while we figure this out."

"So we don't get to keep any of the money?" Brooke asked.

"Not until this is all sorted out," her mother said.

"You should contact your lawyer," Mr. Rodriguez said. Brooke's mom nodded.

Brooke blinked back tears. She'd worked so hard to find the gold and now she couldn't even spend it?

"Do you girls want a ride home?" Brooke's mom asked.

"No, we'll walk," Brooke said. "We have

to tell Mrs. Smith to put back everything we left in the cart."

"I know you're disappointed," her mom said, cupping Brooke's cheek. "I'm sorry."

"Yeah, but hopefully we'll get the gold back soon. Can Izzy stay over again tonight? We'll sleep out in the tree house."

"Of course. See you at home," her mother said.

Brooke noticed Calla just above the door, struggling to fly with several suckers.

Izzy saw too, and they both ran over to her.

"Come hide!" Brooke whispered.

Izzy grabbed the suckers from Calla as the fairy swooped into Brooke's shirt pocket.

"Someone abandoned all those lovely sweet candies! I had to save them," Calla said.

"They're not abandoned," Izzy explained. "They were in a candy jar."

"Ooh. Can you get me a candy jar with your gold?" Calla asked. "Does the candy just multiply in the jar?"

"No, it doesn't work that way." Brooke frowned. "And you'll have to wait to see if we get the gold back."

The girls walked back into the store and got their cart.

"Did you get the money for your gold?" Mrs. Smith asked.

Brooke shook her head. "Mr. Rodriguez thinks the gold is from a bank robbery two hundred years ago."

"Oh, my word!" Mrs. Smith said.

Customers lined up at the cash register whispered excitedly.

"So we're returning all this." Brooke wheeled the cart toward the craft section.

"Thank you," Mrs. Smith said.

It wasn't fun, but Brooke and Izzy put all their treasures back on the store shelves.

When they were done, they stepped outside.

"Now what?" Brooke asked, tired and grumpy from the day's events.

Calla poked her head out of the shirt pocket. "I have several suckers to eat. I'd like to get started on that."

"When we get home," Brooke said.

Izzy snapped her fingers. "I know. Maybe

we can find some information about the robbery at the library. Maybe we can prove it's not the gold from the bank."

Brooke nodded, excited again. They rushed into the library.

"Do you have any information on the bank holdup from 1801?" Brooke asked Mrs. Nelson.

Mrs. Nelson raised her eyebrows. "That's one of the biggest crimes this town ever saw. I'm sure we have something back in the local history section."

The girls hurried to the back of the library and found a book called *The History of Morristown* on display. Brooke plucked it from the shelf, and they sat at a table. Scanning the table of contents, she found an entire chapter on the Boo-Hoo Brothers' bank heist.

Izzy scooted in next to her and Brooke read aloud, *"On a quiet Friday afternoon, two masked men marched into the Morristown Bank holding a rattlesnake. The robbery victims knew they were dealing with the notorious Boo-Hoo Brothers: bandits who cried during their heists.*

"'We've got a deadly rattlesnake and we're not afraid to let him loose!' one of them hollered. Clyde, the brother holding the snake, blubbered and shook as he held the deadly beast.

"His brother, Cletus, whacked him. 'Toughen up, you sissy.'

"'Fine. Then you hold the snake!' Clyde

replied, *shoving the snake toward Cletus as it rattled and twisted in his grip. Then Cletus began to weep in the face of the horrific serpent."*

"Wow!" Izzy said. "How scary."

"I know! There's more: *While the terrified tellers went to retrieve the gold from the vault, the robbers ran around the room with the snake rattling and hissing. The customers huddled on the floor, whimpering and crying, fearing for their lives.*

"An old woman stood and pointed a shaky finger at the brothers. 'Mark my words, from this moment forward, that gold will be cursed until the day it is used for good.'

"'Shut up, old woman,' hollered one of

the brothers as the first teller arrived with two bags.

"But the robbers seemed frightened enough by the curse that they took off with just the two bags instead of waiting for the rest." Brooke paused, her eyes wide.

"I can't believe it!" Izzy said. "I wonder if the curse was real?"

"I don't know. Crazy isn't it?"

Brooke continued with the story.

"No one was injured in the holdup, and the gold was never found. But the Boo-Hoo Brothers suffered a string of misfortunes: Both their horses dropped dead right after the robbery, so they stole a pair from a local farmer. Cletus lost an eye during another holdup. Then their

snake escaped. And while they were hidden on their parents' homestead, lightning hit the home and it burned to the ground. The Boo-Hoo Brothers disappeared and were never heard from again."

"Wow," Izzy whispered. "I wonder if your gold is cursed?"

Brooke felt a shiver shimmy down her spine and closed the book. "I sure hope not."

Chapter 6

Brooke and Izzy brought a picnic dinner up to the tree house. They'd also packed plenty of sweets for Calla and food for the kitties.

The cats quickly ate their meal and found cozy spots in the room.

"You know what *I* would wish for? A lifetime's supply of chocolate chips!" Calla said, taking a break from her lollipop to munch on the new snack.

"I can get that for you once my gold is returned," Brooke promised. "I wonder how long that's going to take?"

"Not too long, I hope," Izzy said.

"You could make another wish while you wait." Calla took a huge bite of the chocolate chip. "Remember, you have only a fortnight! Twelve days left."

Izzy laughed. "You shouldn't talk with your mouth full of chocolate, Calla!"

Calla just shrugged and kept eating.

Brooke sighed. "I have no idea what else I want to wish for. Especially if I don't know whether or not I'll get my gold back."

"Can you imagine being in the bank when the robbers came in?" Izzy said. "How scary."

"Good thing no one got hurt," Brooke said. "If that is the bank's gold, I wonder what happened to the rest of it. Two bags of two hundred coins were stolen. We found only one. Maybe the Boo-Hoo Brothers spent it?"

Izzy jumped up. "Or maybe there's another bag out there! We should dig again tomorrow."

"Great idea! Let's get up early to look," Brooke said.

"There's *got* to be another bag," Izzy said.

"I hope so." The sun was setting, so Brooke stuck the megaphone out the tree-house window and called, "Goodnight, Mom!"

Her mom came out the back door and waved.

"I want to see more wisps," Izzy said. "Maybe they'll come out again tonight." With the binoculars she scanned the forest, looking for the glowing blue creatures. "Now that we know the forest is magical, who knows what we'll see?"

"Elves, gnomes, unicorns," Calla said.

"Ooh, unicorns!" Brooke and Izzy said dreamily.

"And possibly dragons," Calla said.

"Dragons?" Brooke shrieked. "Dragons live in the forest?"

"That's what I've heard. Though I've never seen them. They live in caves deep beneath the earth and sleep for hundreds of years. No one has seen them in a long, long time."

Izzy gulped and set down the binoculars. "So even if they're still around, they're far, far away, right?"

"Oh yes. I think so," Calla said.

"I don't know if I can sleep with all this talk about bank robbers and dragons," Brooke said. "I thought this wish was going to be such an easy one."

Izzy yawned. "Don't worry, everything always looks better in the morning."

Brooke was up just as the sun was rising. "Come on! Let's see if we can find more gold!"

Izzy grabbed the shovel they'd left at the base of the tree, and the girls headed for the creek. But as they got closer, Brooke froze. "Who are all those people?"

Five people were digging holes near the creek. She didn't recognize any of them.

Izzy put her hands on her hips and stomped over to them.

Calla tucked herself in Brooke's pocket, and they followed Izzy.

"Excuse me, what are you doing?" Izzy demanded.

An old man stopped digging and scratched his long, gray beard. "Heard from my cousin that a bag of gold from the holdup was found here yesterday. Said everyone in town was talking about it. I intend to find the other bag."

Brooke was scared to confront these strangers, but they had no right to be here. She tipped up her chin and tried to feel brave. "This is my meadow," she said. "I live right over there. You can't just come in and start digging."

The old man chuckled. "But we already are," he said. "Not sure how you're going to stop us."

The people with him laughed, too, and went back to digging.

Brooke turned away, fighting back tears.

She couldn't believe it—she'd made *another* terrible wish!

Chapter 7

Brooke hurried home and told her mother what was happening in the meadow.

"I don't like this, I don't like this one bit," her mother said, pacing the kitchen. "Maybe you girls shouldn't play out there for a while."

"No!" Brooke cried. "It's our favorite place. Let's tell the police to make everyone go away."

"Fine, but you still have to be careful,"

her mom said. "And come home if you see anything else strange, okay?"

Brooke nodded. She hoped wisps didn't count as "strange."

The girls ran back outside as Brooke's mom called the police. But before any officers showed up, a reporter with a microphone and a man with a camera were there, running toward them.

"Are you the girls who found the gold?" the reporter asked.

Izzy stopped in her tracks and squealed. "TV! We're going to be on TV!"

"Yes," Brooke told the woman, "we found the gold. But now we want everyone to leave. This is my meadow."

"Can you show us where you found it?" the man holding the camera asked.

"Over by the creek, in that big hole," Izzy said. "Are we going to be on TV tonight?"

"You sure are," the reporter said. "This is big news."

The cameraman was busy filming the hole by the creek while Izzy turned circles, still squealing. "We're going to be famous!"

Brooke didn't care one bit. She was too busy examining all the new holes the trespassers had dug. "You're ruining my meadow!" she called to them. "You'd better leave. Police are on the way!"

They all ignored her and kept digging.

Far off in the distance, sirens wailed.

"I told you they were coming," Brooke said.

The group stopped digging and gathered their things, grumbling as they left.

"Those people think there's more gold," Izzy explained to the reporter. "Since the bank robbers took two bags and we found only one."

"Shh!" Brooke hissed.

But the camera was aimed right at them, recording everything Izzy had said.

Brooke pointed at the camera. "We just want people to leave us alone and stop trespassing."

"If you get your gold back from the bank, what are you going to do with it?" the reporter asked. "One and a half million dollars is a lot of money."

"I don't know," Brooke said, worried Calla was going to zoom out of her shirt pocket at any moment. "We've got to go." Brooke dragged Izzy back to the foot of the tree house.

They slumped to the ground and Brooke angrily pulled out handfuls of grass.

"I can't believe those people! This wish has been horrible so far."

Calla climbed out of her pocket and sat on her shoulder. "Wishes aren't always a good thing."

"I know! I thought seven wishes would be the best thing ever." Brooke sighed.

"Don't you want to go back and dig for the other bag?" Izzy asked.

"Maybe later," Brooke said. "There might not even be another bag."

Izzy sighed and leaned against the tree. "Too bad we didn't get those art supplies."

Calla twirled up into the air. "You can make your own paint. That's what we do in Fairvana. The tailors use all kinds of different berries and roots for dyes. We can find some in the forest."

"We're allowed in the magical forest?" Brooke asked.

"Of course," Calla said with a shrug. "It's only enchanted to keep people from *wanting* to go in. But you're not forbidden from entering. Follow me. I'll show you the best things to use."

Brooke and Izzy each grabbed a bucket

and followed Calla. When they reached the creek that separated the meadow from the forest, the girls sloshed through the water.

"I wonder if we'll see any other magical creatures?" Izzy asked.

"You might!" Calla said. "But they might not be happy to see you."

Brooke and Izzy shared a concerned look as they stepped into the dark forest.

The air was much cooler there, and new sounds flooded their ears: high-pitched calls of unknown animals, rustling trees, whooshes of wind.

"We're not going very far, are we?" Brooke asked.

"No, we don't want to disturb the trolls.

Nasty little beasts." Calla fluttered over a bush. "These berries create a beautiful purple color. You'll only need a few."

"Trolls?" Izzy whispered.

Brooke gulped, and placed a handful of berries in her bucket.

Calla zipped over to a different bush. "These leaves will give you a lovely green color."

They wandered through the trees, collecting leaves and bark and roots to create any color they could want.

"These will be perfect to use as canvases," Izzy said, pointing to huge rolls of white bark that had peeled off some birch trees.

Brooke was relieved when they finally

turned back. They hadn't run into a troll . . .
or worse.

But then they heard rustling behind
them, and the distant chatter of voices.
Goose bumps prickled Brooke's skin.
"What's that?" she whispered.

Calla flew above them and darted
between the trees.

Brooke and Izzy held hands, waiting for her to return. "What do you think it could be?" Izzy asked.

"I . . . I . . . don't know," Brooke said, trying not to imagine all the horrible creatures she didn't want to see.

"Where is Calla?" Izzy asked as the rustle of branches and footsteps got closer.

"Found them!" Calla said, swooping down next to the girls.

"Found who?" Brooke asked.

"Leprechauns!" Calla said. "They're coming for the gold!"

Chapter 8

"What should we do?" Brooke asked.

"Nothing," Calla said. "You can't stop lep-rechauns if they're after gold. Well, one thing can stop them, but we don't have to worry about that."

"What is it?" Izzy asked.

But Calla didn't have time to answer, because just then, three men appeared. They were each half the size of Brooke and

Izzy and wearing green suits and shiny black boots.

"I thought I smelled humans in the forest," said one. "Fairy, what are they doing here?"

"They're my guests," Calla said.

One of the men adjusted his little green cap and frowned. "Be sure they do no harm."

"We won't," Brooke said. "We're just gathering roots and berries to make paint."

"We were going to buy paint with the gold we found, but the bank won't let us keep it," Izzy explained.

Brooke slapped her forehead. "Quiet, Izzy!"

"Ah, so you can lead us to the gold," said one of the leprechauns. "I'm McMurtagh.

And this is Hamish and Fitzgibbons. Much obliged for your help."

"Hello, I'm Brooke and this is Izzy," Brooke said, holding out her hand. The little men each grasped her forefinger and shook it, then the same with Izzy.

"I'm sorry, but we can't help you get the gold," Brooke said. "It's locked away in the bank. No one can get it now."

"But you can lead us to the rest," said one of the other little men.

"We don't know if there's any more," Brooke said.

"Aye, there is," said McMurtagh. "We can smell it. We caught a whiff of gold yesterday and started heading this way. We'll be able to find it on our own."

They marched ahead of them out of the woods.

Brooke and Izzy followed Calla as she flew after them.

"But it's not your gold!" Brooke hollered. "It's in *my* meadow. *I* wished for it!"

"Did you, now?" The leprechaun stopped

and planted his hands on his hips. "Well, no matter if you wished for it, found it, or stole it. All gold is originally leprechaun gold and must be returned to us."

"Usually when we smell it, we're too late to retrieve it," said Hamish. "But not this time."

They stepped out of the forest, and the leprechauns leaped over the creek with one jump.

Brooke and Izzy waded through again, trying to keep up with the little men.

They ran across the meadow faster than Brooke could imagine, stooping to sniff the ground, then darting off again. For fifteen minutes, they ran back and forth, shaking their heads, then pointing in a different direction, and running again.

"Maybe they're wrong about another bag of gold being here," Brooke said.

Then one of them stopped by a spot along the creek, farther down from where they'd found the first bag. The leprechaun waved the other two over. They circled around a spot sniffing, and sniffing, then tasting the dirt. "This be the spot!" one of them declared.

They each pulled out a tiny shovel tucked into their belts and started digging, faster than seemed possible.

Brooke and Izzy ran over for a closer look. Within minutes, the leprechauns had dug a deep, wide hole.

Brooke glanced around, hoping no one else was snooping around the meadow.

How in the world would she be able to explain this scene?

"Found it!" one of the leprechauns shouted as he scooped up the bag and jumped out of the hole.

He was holding another bank bag.

"Let's see how much we've got!" one of them said.

They dumped the gold out, and Brooke picked up a coin to see if they were the same as the ones she'd found.

A leprechaun slapped it out of her hand. "That's ours!"

Brooke pulled her hand away. But she'd already seen it was another Turban Head Eagle ten-dollar gold coin. She bent down to examine the bag on the ground.

"Is it Morristown Bank?" Izzy asked.

"Yes," Brooke said.

The leprechauns finished counting. "Two hundred gold coins," Fitzgibbons declared. "Not our best haul but we'll take it."

They scooped the coins back into the bag, and Brooke turned to Calla. "What do we do? Can we stop them?"

"I told you, we can do nothing," Calla said. "Leprechauns have a nasty bite. Turns a human green and hurts like the devil. There's no way you're getting that gold back from three leprechauns."

The little men closed up the bag and brushed their hands together, cleaning off the dirt.

"We thank you very much, Mistress Brooke and Mistress Izzy," said McMurtagh. "We'll be on our way. A good day to you."

Just then a shadow darkened the meadow and the leprechauns screamed, dropped the gold, and sprinted away.

Brooke looked at Calla, confused.

Calla shrieked.

"Dragon! Run!"

Chapter 9

The girls ran as fast as their legs would go, to the closest thing they could hide behind— the big rock in the meadow.

"What does it want?" Brooke asked as she crouched behind the rock, breathless.

"The gold, of course," Calla whispered.

The dragon landed with a thud that shook the ground. It walked around, sniffing the air. "Ah, gold *and* humans," it said in a slow, deep voice.

"What do dragons do to humans?" Izzy whispered.

"I don't know!" Calla said. "It's been ages since a dragon was spotted!"

"I thought I caught a whiff of gold yesterday," the dragon went on. "I can thank those silly leprechauns for digging it up for me."

Brooke was so scared her teeth chattered.

"Come out, come out," the dragon said. "I've already eaten this year. I'm not going to harm you. I need help finding the gold. My eyesight's not so good. Lead me to the gold and I promise not to scorch this lovely field."

"What do we do?" Brooke asked Izzy. But Izzy seemed caught in a daze.

Brooke didn't want to lose her meadow,

so she stood up and walked toward the dragon on shaky legs.

"Be careful!" Calla shouted. "We're friends, remember? I don't want anything bad to happen to you."

"Hello, Mr. Dragon," Brooke managed to say.

The dragon's nostrils flared. "Mister? What makes you think I'm a mister?"

"Um, you're big and scary?"

The dragon laughed. "I'm much bigger and scarier than my brother. And I'm a Miss, if you don't mind."

"I'm s-s-s-sorry," Brooke said.

"Are you part snake?" the dragon asked.

"Nope. Just scared."

The dragon laughed. "Like I said, I've

already eaten. Plus I don't care for humans. I prefer pine trees, charred ever so slightly. Mmm, mmm, good."

Brooke breathed a huge sigh of relief. "Okay. Excellent. I bet they taste very good. I'll have to try one someday. But not one of yours, of course."

"Stop your chitter-chatter, human. Bring me the gold!"

Brooke's legs still wobbled, but she scurried over to the bag of gold and grabbed it. Then she started walking toward the dragon. *Don't drop it, don't drop it*, she told herself.

She stood in front of the enormous green beast. Scales as big as Brooke's head covered her shiny skin. She smelled of smoke

and musty leaves. "Here you go," Brooke said as she crouched to put it on the ground.

"No!" cried the beast, in a voice so loud it rattled Brooke's bones. "I can't see very well. Hand it to me." She raised her front paw, flexing her giant, pointed talons.

Brooke took a deep breath and dropped the bag in her paw. The coins inside clinked as it fell into the dragon's grasp.

"Thank you, human. I must rest now, for at least twenty years. It's been a most eventful day." And she swooped up into the air, the wind from her wings sending Brooke's curls flying.

Brooke plopped onto the ground as the dragon soared over the trees and out of sight.

Izzy and Calla hurried over.

"Right. So to answer your earlier question, *that's* the only thing that can stop leprechauns," Calla said.

"You don't say," Brooke mumbled before passing out.

Chapter 10

Brooke woke to Izzy slapping her cheeks. "Not so hard!" Brooke said.

"Sorry, but you weren't waking up," Izzy said.

"Yeah, I just had a conversation with a dragon. I'm a little stressed out."

Calla was making notes in her journal. "Now I'm a human expert *and* a dragon expert! I'm not sure the fairy folk will believe all that has happened to me."

"See, it wasn't so bad being found by us humans," Brooke said.

"Let's go back to the tree house," Izzy said. "You can rest while we can make our paints."

"Well, I suppose the worst is over, right?" Brooke said as Izzy pulled her back to her feet. "What could be worse than a dragon? I'm starting to think that gold *is* cursed."

Izzy scooped up a bucket of water from the creek, and they climbed back up to the tree house. Brooke felt more relaxed as she made vibrant colors out of the berries, leaves, and water.

Then the girls got their brushes out of the adventure trunk, arranged the pieces of birch bark, and began to paint.

"This is even more fun than painting on canvases!" Izzy said. "I'm glad we couldn't buy all that stuff."

They had enough bark left to make a few NO TRESPASSING signs to post around the meadow.

After hanging up and admiring their

artwork, and then posting the signs, the girls went to Brooke's house for dinner. Brooke dropped a sugar cube into her pocket to keep Calla busy—and quiet. And they set out food for Patches and Pumpkin.

Brooke didn't realize how hungry she was until her mom put the pizza on the table.

"So, did anything else strange happen in the meadow today?" Brooke's mom asked.

Brooke almost choked on a piece of pepperoni.

"Nope," Izzy said. "Nothing strange."

Right, Brooke thought. Strange was not the word for all the things that happened. *Terrifying* and *unbelievable* were more like it.

"Are you sleeping outside again tonight?" her mom asked. "No school tomorrow because of the teacher conference day."

"I almost forgot!" Brooke said.

"Woo-hoo!" Izzy cried.

"Yes, let's sleep outside again. I love the tree house," Brooke said.

"I know. I had so many fun adventures out there as a child, too," her mom said.

"Did you ever see anything unusual?" Brooke asked.

"Like what?" her mom asked.

Brooke shrugged.

"Not that I can remember," her mom said. "Why?"

"Nothing. No reason."

After finishing dessert and grabbing a change of clothes, she and Izzy headed back outside.

"I guess I should start thinking about my next wish," Brooke said. "But I have no idea what I want. I'm worried about getting it wrong again."

"You've still got time before Calla has to leave." Izzy scanned the woods with her binoculars, looking for wisps again. "Wait a minute," she said. "Are wisps ever yellow?"

"No, only blue," Calla said. "Why?"

"Because there are a bunch of yellow lights bobbing around the meadow," Izzy said.

"Let me see." Brooke held out her hand and Izzy gave her the binoculars. She peered out the tree-house window and watched the lights moving, then settling on the ground. Dark figures moved around the field holding long sticks. "Shovels," she said. "More people are here looking for the gold!"

"What are we going to do?" Izzy asked. "The police didn't keep people away. Neither did our signs."

"We should remind them about the curse," Brooke said.

"Yeah, we should scare them," Izzy said.

"Oh! We could make them think the meadow is haunted." Brooke jumped up.

"Awesome idea, but how?"

Brooke thought for a moment. "What do we have up here that could help?"

"We could make scary noises with the megaphone," Izzy suggested.

"Yes! And we could blink our flashlights on and off," Brooke said.

"Oh, oh I know! Calla, do you think the wisps would help us scare everyone away?"

"I could inquire. They do like their mischief." Calla flew to the window and whistled a song. Soon, a group of blue orbs was whizzing their way.

"How are blue lights going to scare them?" Izzy wondered.

Brooke turned back to the fairy. "Calla, could they fly with one of our sheets over them so they look like a ghost?"

"Let's try," Calla said.

Brooke and Izzy held up a sheet, and Calla whistled to the creatures. They zoomed under the white sheet, taking it with them as they flew out the window toward the trespassers.

"That looks really scary!" Izzy said. "In the dark, you can't tell it's a sheet."

Brooke made spooky ghost noises through the megaphone. "Cursed, the gold is cursed," she whispered in a deep, threatening voice. "Anyone who takes it will be cursed as well!"

Izzy covered her face, trying to hold back her giggles.

The dark figures in the meadow stopped digging as the sheet zoomed toward them.

"Let me try it, too!" Calla said. "I'm bigger than the wisps. I can probably carry a sheet all by myself."

Brooke and Izzy held up a sheet for Calla and she flew it toward the people.

"Woooo," Brooke whispered through her megaphone. "Run away. Run away!"

Izzy grabbed the binoculars. "It's working! They're running away!"

The girls high-fived each other as the group fled the meadow. Calla and the wisps soon returned with the sheets.

"Whee! What fun," Calla said as she landed in the tree house. "You humans are trickier than elves!"

"That was great, you guys!" Brooke said to the wisps. "Thank you so much for your help."

The wisps buzzed and chirped with excitement, then zoomed back into the night.

"I hope that's the end of the trespassers," Brooke said. "I wish I could tell them the gold is gone, but who would believe a dragon took it?"

"No one." Izzy collapsed back on a bed. "What an exhausting day."

Brooke fell back next to her. "At least we know not to waste our time digging for more gold."

"Right," Izzy said. "We just have to find a way to get the gold back from the bank."

Chapter 11

Mist swirled through the meadow when they woke up early the next morning. "I'm starving," Brooke said, hurrying through the field.

"Me too!" Calla flew beside her. "Will you be making a new wish today?"

"I don't know. I want to figure out what to do about the gold first," Brooke said.

"We could write a letter to the bank," Izzy said. "Or march in front of it with protest signs?"

"Those are both good ideas," Brooke said—right before she tripped in a hole and tumbled to the ground. "Oww! My ankle!"

Izzy knelt beside her. "Someone must have dug this last night. Can you walk back home with my help?"

"I'll try," Brooke whimpered. "Oh, there are holes everywhere! How many people were out here digging? My meadow is ruined!"

Izzy helped Brooke up. Brooke winced and slung one arm over Izzy's shoulder. They limped back to Brooke's house.

"Should I get in your pocket?" Calla asked.

"No, my mom might see you while she's looking at my ankle."

Izzy lifted her hair up and pointed to the collar of her hoodie. "You can hide under here."

Calla flew onto her shoulder, and Izzy let her hair fall back in place. Calla giggled. "That tickles."

"You have to be quiet!" Izzy warned.

Brooke's mom was cooking at the stove when they walked in. She looked up as the girls walked in. "Hungry?" Then her eyes widened. "What happened?" She rushed over to Brooke.

"There are holes all over the meadow and I fell in one. My ankle hurts so much!" Brooke couldn't hold back the tears.

"We need to go to the hospital right away," Brooke's mom said.

"Can I come?" Izzy asked. "I want to be sure she's okay."

"Of course, dear."

Izzy snatched a sugar cube for Calla before they climbed in the car. Brooke's mom quickly drove to the emergency room.

Luckily, an X-ray showed it was just a sprain, so a doctor wrapped Brooke's ankle and told her she should feel better in a few days.

"That's a relief," Brooke said on the drive home. Her bad luck *had* to be behind her now!

But when they got home, two men in suits were standing at the front door.

"Can I help you?" Brooke's mom asked.

"I'm representing family members of the Boo-Hoo Brothers. They're making a legal claim to the gold," one man said.

The other man held out an envelope, too. "And I'm representing the family of the former owner of this land. They believe the gold should be theirs."

They went inside and Brooke slumped on the couch. "What does this mean, Mom?"

Her mom sat next to her. "It means the case over who gets the gold will be tied up in court for a very long time. And I hate to say it, but I don't know if I can afford the legal fees to fight for it. Even if we do win, we'd owe a very big lawyer bill."

Brooke wanted to go out in the meadow and scream.

Her mom patted her leg. "Everything will be fine."

But Brooke didn't believe her. So many bad things had happened since she had found that gold.

"Let's go outside," Izzy said. "I'll help you fill in all the holes in the meadow."

Brooke nodded.

"Be very careful," her mom said.

"We will."

As they slowly walked outside, Brooke said, "I wish I'd never made that wish."

Calla flew out from under Izzy's hoodie. "Sorry, you aren't permitted to make such a wish. I can't undo what's been done."

Brooke sighed. "I know. I wasn't actually making a wish. I'm just worried I'm going to be cursed forever because of that gold."

"Remember what the article said? The curse will be in effect until the gold is used for good?" Izzy asked.

"And what good is it doing locked in a box in the bank?" Brooke asked.

Izzy shrugged. "It's too bad you couldn't

tell the lawyers you don't want it. That they should do something good with it instead."

Brooke thought about what good all that money could do, and then the perfect solution popped right into her brain. "Izzy, I think I know the answer!"

Chapter 12

Brooke's mom made a few phone calls, and the lawyers for everyone trying to claim the gold met them at the bank. They sat down at a big table in a conference room.

Mr. Rodriguez stood up. "Brooke, your mother says you girls have a proposal."

Brooke cleared her throat, standing up as tall as she could. "We do. My mom explained this is going to cost everybody a lot of money to pay their lawyers to fight for this. And only one of us is going to win."

There was some mumbling and nodding around the table.

"Indeed," Mr. Rodriguez said. "It could take years to sort this out."

"Right," Brooke said. "And there's the matter of the curse. You might not know, but during the robbery, an old woman cast a spell, saying the gold will be cursed until the day it's used for good. Let me tell you, I have been cursed for sure since I found it. My meadow is destroyed, I sprained my ankle, and I lost the darn gold." She did not mention the leprechaun and dragon incidents. "I have so many good things in my life already, like a beautiful meadow, and a tree house, and a very best friend. I don't need the gold."

"So what do you propose?" asked Mr. Rodriguez.

"The library really needs donations. Mrs. Nelson says things are bad. She couldn't even buy any new books this year. I'm worried the library might close. So I say we donate the money to the library. All of it. That would certainly be good use of the gold, and hopefully break the curse."

Eyebrows raised around the table.

"It sounds like a wonderful idea to me. What do you think?" Mr. Rodriguez asked the two lawyers.

"Give us a few minutes to contact our clients," one of them said.

Mr. Rodriguez grinned. "I think it would be a perfect ending for this long-lost gold."

"I think so, too," Brooke said, crossing her fingers.

Mr. Rodriguez and the lawyers left the room and Brooke looked over at Izzy. "No fancy beds for us or the cats."

Izzy shrugged. "That's okay. My favorite place to sleep is the tree house, and a fancy bed would be silly in there. And we didn't even need the craft supplies. We made our own."

Brooke sighed. "Another wasted wish."

"I don't think it was wasted," Izzy said.

"We saw leprechauns and a dragon, and the library will get all the money."

Brooke smiled. "That's true. You always find a way to make things seem better. Thanks! I couldn't wish for a better friend."

Izzy beamed.

The grown-ups filed back into the room and Mr. Rodriguez held out his hands. "Brooke, you have a deal. We'll donate all the gold to the library. But first, we have some business to finish with you."

Chapter 13

Brooke was confused. "What?"

"There's the matter of the reward. The Federal Bank of Morristown promised one hundred dollars for return of the gold. Seems like you found what was left, so the bank wants to present you with one hundred dollars in cash."

Izzy pumped her fist in the air and Brooke cried, "Oh my gosh!"

Mr. Rodriguez handed Brooke a crisp

one-hundred-dollar bill. "Maybe you can go back to the store and buy those things you wanted the other day."

"Thank you so much!" Brooke said.

"No, thank you. For finding the gold and for suggesting such a wonderful solution for how to use it," Mr. Rodriguez said.

Brooke and Izzy hurried over to the store, though Brooke's limp slowed them down a bit.

Mrs. Smith was there to greet them. "Girls! Did you finally get your gold to spend?"

"No, but we did get a reward for finding it!" Brooke said, waving the one-hundred-dollar bill.

"Wonderful! I've got a metal detector if you'd like to buy that and look for more," Mrs. Smith suggested.

"No, thanks!" Brooke and Izzy said at the same time.

Laughing, they went to the toy aisle and got Calla some new dollhouse furniture. Then they got some snacks for a picnic. They even had enough money for two fancy cat beds.

"Forty-two dollars left," Brooke said. "We can each put twenty-one dollars in our piggy banks, since we spent all our money on cat food the other day."

"Thanks so much!" Izzy said, stuffing the money in her pocket.

When they walked out of the store, Mrs. Nelson was coming down the steps of the library.

"Come here, you wonderful girls!" When they reached her, Mrs. Nelson gave them both big hugs. "I just heard from Mr. Rodriguez. What an amazing thing you've done for the library."

"We wanted to spend some of the gold on new books," Brooke said, "but it's just as good if you can buy books for the library. We can borrow them anytime, and so can everyone else."

"I just have one problem," Mrs. Nelson said.

"What?" Brooke asked, confused.

"I have so much money to spend on new

books, I'm not exactly sure what to get. I'd like you both to help me choose some."

"Really?" Izzy asked. "Wow!"

Mrs. Nelson nodded. "Any suggestions?"

Brooke thought about what books she'd like to read, what subjects she'd like to learn more about. "How about some books on dragons? And leprechauns?"

Izzy smirked. "And lots of books about fairies."

Mrs. Nelson tilted her head. "I find that surprising."

"Why?" Brooke asked.

"You two usually like nonfiction books, like all the books on cats you checked out, or the one on the town's history. Books that can teach you something about the real world, not fictional creatures."

Brooke could feel Calla stirring, so she poked her pocket to keep her quiet. She smiled. "Oh, I think we'll enjoy them anyway."

Brooke and Izzy headed down to the pond for their celebration picnic. They tossed bread to the geese, who honked in appreciation for the snack.

Calla sat in the grass braiding tiny daisies together. "I don't know why you need books to learn about fairies," Calla said. "Ask me anything."

"I'm hoping for books to help me make a better wish!" Brooke joked.

"You've got four wishes left to get it right,"

Calla said. "Maybe you should stop wishing for *things*."

Brooke thought for a minute. She had wished for a hundred cats, and long-lost gold. What could she wish for that wasn't a thing? Then she got a great idea.

"Oh! I think you're right. I think I have a perfectly wonderful wish that couldn't possibly hurt anyone. Calla, I wish for . . ."

The magic continues...
Turn the page for a sneak peek at

#3 Perfectly Popular

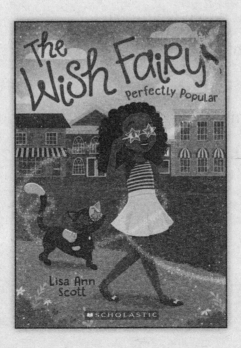

Brooke had four more wishes to make. And she was determined not to mess things up again.

"I've decided I'm done wishing for *stuff*," Brooke told Izzy and Calla.

"This sounds interesting," Calla said.

"I'm confused." Izzy laughed. "What are you going to wish for, then?"

Brooke grinned up at the sun. "Something special. Something you can't buy. Something I'll be so proud of. I should really be using these wishes to make my life better, not just to *get* things, you know?"

"That sounds awesome." Izzy jumped up, scattering the tiny flowers she'd been picking. "What would make your life better?" She held out a hand and pulled Brooke up from the ground.

"I'm tired of being invisible," Brooke said, brushing off her shorts. "I want everyone at school to know who I am."

"You know how to turn invisible?" Calla asked. "I can't even do that."

Brooke laughed. "No, I mean most people never even notice me. I want to change that."

"How can you make that happen?" Izzy asked.

"I think I know. But first, I have to get the wording right." Brooke rehearsed the wish in her head. For her last wish, she'd asked for buried gold to appear in her meadow—but when the wish came true, the gold was still buried! It took a long time to find it.

So, perfect wording was a must when making wishes. She took a deep breath.

Welcome 21982318597600

ENCHANTED PONY ACADEMY,

where dreams sparkle and magic shines!